RIP VAN WINKLE or the
Strange Men
of the Mountains

LEGEND OF SLEEPY HOLLOW or the
Headless Horseman

by WASHINGTON IRVING

Edited by Sandra Sanders

Illustrations by William Hogarth

SCHOLASTIC INC.
New York Toronto London Auckland Sydney Tokyo

ISBN 0-590-40110-6

12 11 10 9 8 7 6 5 4 3   8 9/8 0/9

Contents

RIP VAN WINKLE or
The Strange Men of the Mountains

The Enchanted Mountains

WHOEVER has made a voyage up the Hudson must remember the Catskill Mountains. They are seen away to the west of the river, swelling up to a noble height, and lording it over the surrounding country.

Every change of season, every change of weather, indeed every hour of the day produces some change in the magical hues and shapes of these mountains; and they are regarded by all the good wives, far and near, as perfect barometers.

At the foot of these fairy mountains, the traveler may have seen the light smoke curling up from the chimneys of a village whose shingle roofs gleam among the trees just where the blue tints of the upland melt away into the fresh green of the nearer landscape. It is a little village of great antiquity, having been founded by some of the Dutch colonists in early times, just about the beginning of the government of the good Peter Stuyvesant (may he rest in peace!). Some of the houses of the original settlers were still standing there, built of small yellow bricks brought from Holland, with latticed windows and gable fronts, and surmounted with weathercocks.

Rip Van Winkle and His Scolding Wife

In that same village, and in one of these very houses (which, to tell the precise truth, was sadly timeworn and weatherbeaten) there lived, many years since, while the country was yet a province of Great Britain, a simple good-natured fellow by the name of Rip Van Winkle. He was a kind neighbor and an obedient, henpecked husband. Indeed, it was his meekness of spirit which gained him such universal popularity; for men who are married to shrews are apt to be gentle and easy to get along with. Their tempers, doubtless, are softened in the fiery furnace of a troubled home. A nagging wife may therefore, in some respects, be a blessing. If so, Rip was thrice blessed.

Certain it is that he was a great favorite among all the good wives of the village. They took his part in all family squabbles, and when gossiping, never failed to lay all the blame on Dame Van Winkle.

The children of the village, too, would shout with joy whenever Rip approached. He joined in their sports, made their playthings, taught them to fly kites and shoot marbles, and told them long stories of ghosts, witches, and Indians. As he went dodging about the village, he was surrounded by a troop of them hanging on his coattails, clambering on his back, and playing a thousand tricks on him; and not a dog would bark at him throughout the neighborhood.

Rip's great fault was that he detested all kinds of profitable labor. It was not that he could not stick to a task. He would sit on a wet rock, with a long and heavy rod, and fish all day without a murmur, even when he was not encouraged by a single nibble. He would carry a gun on his shoulder for hours together, trudging through woods and swamps, and up hill and down dale, to shoot a few squirrels or wild pigeons. He would never refuse to assist a neighbor even in the roughest toil, and was a foremost man at all county frolics for husking Indian corn, or building stone fences. The women of the village, too, used to employ him to run their errands, and to do such little odd jobs as their husbands would not do for them. In a word, Rip was ready to attend to anybody's business but his own. As to doing family duty and keeping his farm in order, he found it impossible.

In fact, he declared it was of no use to work on his farm; it was the worst little piece of ground in the whole country; everything about it went wrong, and would go wrong in spite of him. His fences were continually falling to pieces; his cow would go astray, or get among the cabbages; weeds were sure to grow quicker in his fields than anywhere else; the rain always made a point of setting in just as he had some outdoor work to do. The estate his father had left him had dwindled away under Rip's management, acre by acre, until there was little more left than a mere patch of Indian corn and potatoes. Yet even that small farm was the worst-conditioned in the neighborhood.

His children, too, were as ragged and wild as if they belonged to nobody. His son, Rip, looked just like him and promised to inherit the habits, as well as the old clothes, of his father. He was generally seen trooping like a colt at his mother's heels, dressed in a pair of his father's castoff trousers which he had to hold up with one hand, as a fine lady does her train in bad weather.

Rip Van Winkle, however, was one of those happy, foolish men who take the world easy, eat white bread or brown — whichever can be got with least thought or trouble — and would rather starve on a penny than work for a dollar.

If left to himself, Rip would have whistled life away, in perfect contentment. But his wife kept continually dinning in his ears about his idleness, his carelessness, and the ruin he was bringing on his family. Morning, noon, and night, her tongue was always going, and everything he said or did was sure to bring forth a storm of words.

—Rip had but one way of replying to all her lectures. He shrugged his shoulders, shook his head, cast up his eyes, but said nothing. This, however, always provoked a fresh volley from his wife, so that Rip would often take to the outside of the house — the only side which belongs to a henpecked husband.

Rip's best friend was his dog, Wolf, who was as much henpecked as his master; for Dame Van Winkle regarded them as companions in idleness. She even looked upon Wolf with an evil eye as the cause of his master's going so often astray. The dog was as courageous an animal as ever scoured the woods — but what courage can withstand the ever-doing and all-besetting terrors of a woman's tongue? The moment Wolf entered the house, his crest fell, his tail drooped to the ground, or curled between his legs. He sneaked about with a gallows air, casting many a sidelong glance at Dame Van Winkle, and at the least flourish of a broomstick or ladle, he would fly to the door with yelping haste.

At the Inn

Times grew worse and worse for Rip Van Winkle as the years of married life rolled on. A tart temper never mellows with age, and a sharp tongue is the only tool that grows keener with constant use.

When he was driven from home, Rip would pass the time with a group of idle men who gathered on a bench before a small inn — an inn which was known by a large sign hanging over the street, a portrait of King George the Third. Here the men used to sit in the shade through a long, lazy summer's day, talking over village gossip, or telling endless sleepy stories about nothing.

But it would have been worth any statesman's money to have heard the profound discussions which sometimes took place, when by chance an old newspaper fell into their hands from some passing traveler. How solemnly they would listen to the contents as drawled out by Derrick Van Brummel, the schoolmaster, a dapper learned little man, who was not to be daunted by the most gigantic word in the dictionary. How sagely the men would deliberate upon public events — some months after they had taken place.

The opinions of this group were completely controlled by Nicholas Vedder, one of the oldest men in the village and landlord of the inn. From morning till night he sat by the door, just moving sufficiently to avoid the sun and keep in the shade of a large tree; so that by his movements the neighbors could tell the hour as accurately as by a sundial. It is true he was rarely heard to speak, but just sat and smoked his pipe. His followers, however (for every great man has his followers), perfectly understood him and could tell what he was thinking. When anything that was read or told displeased him, he would smoke his pipe with short, frequent, angry puffs. But when pleased, he would inhale the smoke slowly and tranquilly, and let it out in light and placid clouds. Sometimes, taking the pipe from his mouth and letting the smoke curl about his nose, he would gravely nod his head in token of perfect approval.

From even this stronghold the unlucky Rip was at length routed by his shrewish wife. She would suddenly break in upon the peaceful crowd and scold all the members. Not even Nicholas Vedder was safe from her tongue, and she charged him outright with encouraging her husband in habits of idleness.

Off to the Woods

Poor Rip was at last reduced almost to despair; and the only way he could escape from the labor of the farm and the clamor of his wife was to take a gun in hand and stroll into the woods. Here he would sometimes seat himself at the foot of a tree, and share the contents of his pack with Wolf, whom he looked upon as a fellow sufferer. "Poor Wolf," he would say, "thy mistress leads thee a dog's life of it; but never mind, my lad, whilst I live thou shalt never be in want of a friend to stand by thee!" Wolf would wag his tail, look wistfully in his master's face, and I truly believe he pitied Rip with all his heart.

In one of their long rambles, on a fine autumnal day, Rip had unconsciously scrambled to one of the highest parts of the Catskill Mountains. He was after his favorite sport of squirrel-shooting, and the lonely silence had echoed and re-echoed with the reports of his gun. Panting and tired out, he threw himself, late in the afternoon, on a green knoll, covered with mountain herbage, that perched at the edge of a cliff. From an opening between the trees he could overlook all the lower country for many a mile of rich woodland. He saw at a distance the lordly Hudson, far, far below him, moving on its silent, majestic course, with the reflection of a purple cloud or the sail of a boat here and there sleeping on its glassy bosom, and at last losing itself in the blue highlands.

On the other side Rip looked down into a deep mountain glen, wild, lonely, and shagged. The bottom, filled with fragments from the surrounding cliffs, was scarcely lighted by the reflected rays of the setting sun. For some time Rip lay musing on this scene. Evening was gradually advancing, and the mountains began to throw their long blue shadows over the valleys. Rip saw that it would be dark long before he could reach the village; and he heaved a heavy sigh when he thought of going home to the terrors of Dame Van Winkle.

The Strange Men of the Mountain

As Rip was about to start down the mountain, he heard a voice from a distance hallooing: "Rip Van Winkle! Rip Van Winkle!" He looked around, but could see nothing but a crow winging its solitary flight across the mountain. He thought his mind must have played a trick on him, and turned again to go down, when he heard the same cry ring through the still, evening air: "Rip Van Winkle! Rip Van Winkle!" At the same time Wolf bristled up his back, and giving a low growl, he skulked to his master's side, looking fearfully down into the glen. Rip now felt a vague uneasiness stealing over him. He looked anxiously in the same direction, and made out a strange figure slowly toiling up the rocks, and bending under the weight of something he carried on his back. Rip was surprised to see any human being in this lonely place, but supposing it to be someone of the neighborhood in need of his assistance, he hastened down to help.

On nearer approach, he was still more surprised at the oddness of the stranger's appearance. The man was a short, square-built old fellow with thick bushy hair and a grizzled beard. His clothing was of the Dutch fashion of many years before — a cloth jerkin strapped around the waist, and several pairs of breeches, the outer one of ample volume, decorated with rows of buttons down the sides, and bunches at the knee. He bore on his shoulders a stout keg that seemed full of liquor, and he made signs for Rip to approach and assist him with the load. Though rather shy and distrustful of this new acquaintance, Rip hurried to help as he always did. So, first, one carrying the keg and then the other, they clambered up a narrow gully, apparently the dry bed of a mountain stream.

As they climbed, Rip, every now and then, heard long rolling peals, like distant thunder, that seemed to issue out of a deep ravine, or rather cleft between lofty rocks, toward which their rugged path led.

Rip paused for an instant, but supposing it to be the muttering of one of those brief thundershowers which often take place in the mountain heights, he proceeded.

Passing through the ravine, they came to a hollow, like a small amphitheatre, surrounded by high cliffs, over the brinks of which trees shot their branches, so that you only caught glimpses of the azure sky, and the bright evening cloud. During the whole time, Rip and his companion had labored on in silence. Rip marveled greatly at what could be the object of carrying a keg of liquor up this wild mountain, yet there was something strange about the unknown that inspired awe and kept him silent.

On entering the amphitheatre, new objects of wonder presented themselves. On a level spot in the center was a company of odd-looking men playing at ninepins. They were dressed in quaint, outlandish fashion. Some wore short doublets, others jerkins, with long knives in their belts, and most of them had enormous breeches, similar to the guide's.

Their faces, too, were peculiar. One had a large head, broad face, and small piggish eyes. The face of another seemed to consist entirely of nose, and was topped by a white sugar-loaf hat, set off with a little red cock's tail. They all had beards, of various shapes and colors. There was one who seemed to be the commander. He was a stout old gentleman with a weather-beaten face. He wore a laced doublet, broad belt and short sword, high-crowned hat and feather, red stockings, and high-heeled shoes with roses on them. The whole group reminded Rip of the figures in an old Flemish painting that hung in the parlor of Dominie Van Shaick, the village parson. The picture had been brought over from Holland at the time the town had been settled.

What seemed particularly odd to Rip was that, though these folks were evidently amusing themselves, they maintained the gravest faces, and the most mysterious silence. They were, withal, the most melancholy party he had ever witnessed. Nothing interrupted the stillness of the scene but the noise of the balls, which, whenever they were rolled, echoed along the mountains like rumbling peals of thunder.

As Rip and his companion approached, the group suddenly stopped their play and stared at Rip with such a fixed statuelike gaze, and such strange, lack-luster eyes, that his heart turned within him, and his knees began to knock. His companion now emptied the contents of the keg into large flagons, and made signs to him to serve the company. Rip obeyed with fear and trembling. They downed the liquor in profound silence and then returned to their game.

By degrees, Rip's awe and fear quieted. He even ventured, when no eye was fixed upon him, to taste the beverage, which he found had a fine flavor. He was naturally a thirsty soul, and was soon tempted to drink again. One taste provoked another; and he went back to the flagon so often that at length his senses were overpowered, his eyes swam in his head, his head gradually declined, and he fell into a deep sleep.

Rip Awakes

On waking, Rip found himself on the green knoll whence he had first seen the old man of the glen. He rubbed his eyes — it was a bright sunny morning. The birds were hopping and twittering among the bushes, and an eagle was wheeling aloft, breasting the pure mountain breeze.

"Surely," thought Rip, "I have not slept here all night!"

He recalled what had happened before he fell asleep. The strange man with the keg of liquor — the mountain ravine — the wild retreat among the rocks — the woeful party at ninepins — the flagon of liquor —

"Oh, that flagon! That wicked flagon!" thought Rip. "What excuse shall I make to Dame Van Winkle?"

He looked around for his gun, but in place of the clean, well-oiled fowling piece he had brought the day before, he found an old one lying by him. The barrel was encrusted with rust, the lock falling off, and the stock worm-eaten. Rip now suspected that the strange men of the mountain had tricked him; having dosed him with liquor, they had robbed him of his gun. Wolf, too, had disappeared, but he

might have strayed away after a squirrel or a partridge. Rip whistled after him and shouted his name, but all in vain; the echoes repeated his whistle and shout, but no dog was to be seen.

Rip determined to revisit the scene of the last evening's party, and if he met with any of the men, to demand his dog and gun. As he rose to walk, he found himself stiff in the joints, and without his usual energy.

"These mountain beds do not agree with me," thought Rip, "and if this foolish adventure should lay me up with a fit of rheumatism, I shall have a blessed time with Dame Van Winkle."

With some difficulty, he got down into the glen. He found the gully which he and his companion had climbed up the evening before; but to his astonishment a mountain stream was now foaming down it, leaping from rock to rock, and filling the glen with babbling murmurs. Rip managed to scramble up its sides, working his toilsome way through thickets of birch, sassafras, and witch hazel; and sometimes tripped up or entangled by the wild grapevines that twisted their coils or tendrils from tree to tree and spread a kind of network in his path.

At length he reached the spot where the ravine had opened through the cliffs to the amphitheatre, but no traces of such opening remained. The rocks presented a high impassable wall, over which the stream came tumbling in a sheet of feathery foam and fell into a broad deep basin, black from the shadows of the surrounding forest. Here, then, poor Rip was brought to a standstill. He again called and whistled after his dog. His only answer was the cawing of a flock of idle crows, sporting high in the air about a dry tree that overhung a sunny cliff.

What was to be done? The morning was passing away, and Rip felt famished for want of his breakfast. He grieved to give up his dog and gun. He dreaded to meet his wife, but it would not do to starve among the mountains. He shook his head, shouldered the rusty firelock, and with a heart full of trouble and anxiety, turned his steps homeward.

Rip Returns Home

As he approached the village, he met a number of people, but none whom he knew, which somewhat surprised him, for he had thought he knew everyone in the country round. Their dress, too, was of a different fashion from what he was used to. They all stared at him with equal marks of surprise, and whenever they cast their eyes upon him stroked their chins. At last Rip, involuntarily, did the same, and to his astonishment, he found his beard had grown a foot long!

He had now entered the outskirts of the village. A troop of strange children ran at his heels, hooting after him, and pointing at his gray beard. The dogs, too, not one of which he recognized, barked at him as he passed. The very village was changed: it was larger and there were more people. There were rows of houses which he had never seen be-

fore, and those he had known had disappeared.
Strange names were over the doors — strange
faces at the windows — everything was strange.

He couldn't believe his eyes. He began to doubt
whether both he and the world around him were not
bewitched. Surely this was his native village, which
he had left but the day before. There stood the Catskill Mountains — there ran the silver Hudson at a
distance — there was every hill and dale precisely
as it had always been — Rip was sorely perplexed.

"That flagon last night," thought he, "has addled
my poor head sadly!"

It was with some difficulty that he found the way
to his own house. He approached with silent awe,
expecting every moment to hear the shrill voice of
Dame Van Winkle. He found the house gone to
decay — the roof fallen in, the windows shattered,
and the doors off the hinges. A half-starved dog, that
looked like Wolf, was skulking about it. Rip called
him by name, but the cur snarled, showed his teeth,
and passed on. This was an unkind cut indeed.
"My very dog," sighed poor Rip, "has forgotten me!"

He entered the house, which, to tell the truth, Dame Van Winkle had always kept in neat order. It was empty, forlorn, and apparently abandoned. This emptiness overcame all his fears of Dame Van Winkle — he called loudly for his wife and children. The lonely rooms rang for a moment with his voice, and then all again was silent.

He now hurried out and hastened to the village inn — but it, too, was gone. A large rickety wooden building stood in its place, with great gaping windows, some of them broken, and mended with old hats and petticoats, and over the door was painted, "The Union Hotel, by Jonathan Doolittle."

Instead of the great tree that used to shelter the quiet little Dutch inn of yore, there now was a tall naked pole, with something on the top that looked like a red nightcap, and from it was fluttering a flag, on which was a strange arrangement of stars and stripes. All this was impossible to understand.

Rip recognized on the sign, however, the ruby face of King George, under which he had smoked many a peaceful pipe. Yet even this was different. The red coat was changed for one of blue and buff. A sword was held in the hand instead of a scepter, the head was decorated with a cocked hat, and underneath was painted in large characters, "General Washington."

There was, as usual, a crowd of folk about the door, but none that Rip recalled. The very character of the people seemed changed. There was a busy, bustling tone about the inn, instead of the usual quiet and drowsy peacefulness. He looked in vain for old Nicholas Vedder, with his broad face, double chin, and fair long pipe, uttering clouds of tobacco-smoke instead of idle speeches. Or for Van Brummel, the schoolmaster, reading out the contents of an ancient newspaper. In place of these friends, a lean pinched-looking fellow with his pockets full of handbills was giving a loud speech about rights of citizens — elections — members of Congress — liberty — Bunker Hill — heroes of seventy-six — and other words, which were perfect nonsense to the bewildered Van Winkle.

The appearance of Rip, with his long, grizzled beard, his rusty fowling piece, his rough dress, and an army of women and children at his heels, soon attracted the attention of the tavern politicians. They crowded around him, eyeing him from head to foot with great curiosity. The speaker bustled up to him, and drawing him partly aside, inquired on which side he voted. Rip stared in vacant stupidity. Another short but busy little fellow pulled him by the arm, and rising on tiptoe, inquired in his ear whether he was Federal or Democrat. Rip was equally at a loss to understand the question.

Then a knowing, self-important old gentleman, in a sharp cocked hat, made his way through the crowd, putting them to the right and left with his elbows as he passed. Planting himself before Van Winkle, with one hand on his hip, and the other resting on his cane, his keen eyes seemed to bore into Rip's very soul. In a stern voice he demanded to know what had brought him to the election with a gun on his shoulder, and a mob at his heels; and whether he meant to breed a riot in the village.

"Alas, gentlemen!" cried Rip, somewhat dismayed, "I am a poor, quiet man, a native of this town, and a loyal subject of the King, God bless him!"

Here a general shout burst from the bystanders — "A spy! A spy! Away with him!" It was with great difficulty that the self-important man in the cocked hat restored order. And now, looking ten times as stern as before, he demanded again of the unknown old man what he came there for, and whom he was seeking. Poor Rip humbly assured him that he meant no harm, but merely came there in search of some of his neighbors who used to come to the tavern.

"Well — who are they? Name them."

Rip bethought himself a moment, and inquired, "Where's Nicholas Vedder?"

There was a silence for a little while, when an old man replied in a thin, piping voice, "Nicholas Vedder? Why, he is dead and gone these eighteen years. There was a wooden tombstone in the church-yard that used to tell all about him, but that's rotten and gone, too."

"Where's Brom Dutcher?"

"Oh, he went off to the army in the beginning of the war. Some say he was killed at the storming of Stony Point — others say he was drowned in a

squall at the foot of Antony's Nose. I don't know —
he never came back again."

"Where's Van Brummel, the schoolmaster?"

"He went off to the war, too; was a great militia
general, and is now in Congress."

Rip's heart died away at hearing of these sad
changes in his home and friends, and at finding himself thus alone in the world. Every answer puzzled
him. Why did they all speak of such a long passage
of time, and other matters which he could not understand: war — Congress — Stony Point? He had
no courage to ask about any more of his friends,
but cried out in despair, "Does nobody here know
Rip Van Winkle?"

"Oh, Rip Van Winkle!" exclaimed two or three.
"Oh, to be sure! That's Rip Van Winkle yonder,
leaning against the tree."

Rip looked, and beheld a man who looked exactly
like himself on the day he went up the mountain:
apparently as lazy, and certainly as ragged. Poor Rip
was now completely confounded. He doubted who
he was, whether he was himself or another man. In
the midst of his bewilderment, the man in the cocked
hat demanded who he was, and what was his name?

"God knows!" exclaimed Rip, at his wit's end.
"I'm not myself — I'm somebody else — that's
me yonder — no — that's somebody else, got into

my shoes. I was myself last night, but I fell asleep on the mountains, and they've changed my gun, and everything's changed, and I'm changed, and I can't tell what's my name, or who I am!"

The bystanders began now to look at each other, nod, wink, and tap their fingers against their foreheads. There was a whisper, also, about getting his gun and keeping the old fellow from doing mischief. At this suggestion, the self-important man with the cocked hat stepped back hastily.

Rip Makes a Discovery

At this critical moment a fresh, pretty woman pressed through the throng to get a peep at the gray-bearded man. She had a chubby child in her arms, who, frightened at Rip's looks, began to cry. "Hush, Rip," cried the woman. "Hush, you little fool; the old man won't hurt you." The name of the child, the air of the mother, the tone of her voice, all awakened a train of recollection in Rip's mind.

"What is your name, my good woman?" asked he.

"Judith Gardenier."

"And your father's name?"

"Ah, poor man, Rip Van Winkle was his name, but it's twenty years since he went away from home with his gun, and never has been heard of since. His dog came home without him; but whether he shot himself, or was carried away by the Indians, nobody can tell. I was then but a little girl."

Rip had but one more question to ask; but he put it with a faltering voice:

"Where's your mother?"

"Oh, she, too, died, but a short time since."

It seemed that she broke a blood vessel in a fit of anger at a New England peddler.

There was a drop of comfort, at least, in this news. The honest man could contain himself no longer. He caught his daughter and her child in his arms.

"I am your father!" cried he. "Young Rip Van Winkle once — old Rip Van Winkle now. Does nobody know poor Rip Van Winkle!"

All stood amazed, until an old woman, tottering out from the crowd, put her hand to her brow, and peering under it in his face for a moment, exclaimed, "Sure enough! It is Rip Van Winkle — it is himself. Welcome home again, old neighbor. Why, where have you been all these twenty long years?"

Rip's story was soon told, for the whole twenty years had been to him but as one night. The neighbors stared when they heard it. Some were seen to wink at each other, and put their tongues in their cheeks. As for the self-important man in the cocked hat, now that the alarm was over, he came near to Rip again, screwed down the corners of his mouth, and shook his head — upon which there was a general shaking of heads throughout the crowd.

It was determined, however, to ask the opinion of old Peter Vanderdonk, who was seen slowly advancing up the road. He was related to a historian who had written one of the earliest accounts of that region. Peter was the oldest man in the village, and knew all the wonderful events and traditions of the neighborhood.

He remembered Rip at once, and said his story was true. He assured the company that it was a fact that the Catskill Mountains had always been haunted by strange beings, and that the great Hendrick Hudson, the first discoverer of the river and country, appeared every twenty years, with his crew of the *Half-Moon,* to revisit the scenes he had known and to keep an eye upon the river and the town called by his name. His father had once seen them in their old Dutch clothes, playing at ninepins in a hollow of the mountain. And he himself had heard, one summer afternoon, the sound of their balls, like distant peals of thunder.

To make a long story short, the company broke up and returned to the more important concerns of the election. Rip's daughter took Rip home to live with her. She had a snug, well-furnished house, and a stout cheery farmer for a husband, whom Rip remembered as one of the children who used to climb upon his back. As to Rip's son, who was the ditto of himself, seen leaning against the tree, he was employed to work on the farm; but like his father, he attended to everything else but his own duties.

Rip now resumed his old walks and habits. He soon found many of his former friends, though all rather the worse for the wear and tear of time. In fact, he preferred making friends among the younger generation, with whom he soon grew into great favor.

Having nothing to do at home, and being arrived at that happy age when a man is allowed to be idle, he took his place once more on the bench at the inn door, and was looked up to as one of the elders of the village, and a teller of tales about the old times

"before the war." It was some time before Rip could get into the regular track of gossip, or could be made to understand the strange events that had taken place while he slept: that there had been a Revolutionary War — that the country had thrown off the yoke of old England — and that, instead of being a subject of His Majesty George the Third, he was now a free citizen of the United States.

Rip, in fact, was no politician; the changes of states and empires made but little impression on him. The only kind of government that had ever made him unhappy was — petticoat government. Happily, that was at an end. He had gotten his neck out of the yoke of matrimony, and could go in and out whenever he pleased without dreading the rule of Dame Van Winkle. Whenever her name was mentioned, however, Rip shook his head, shrugged his shoulders, and cast up his eyes; which might pass either for an expression of sadness or of joy.

He used to tell his story to every stranger that arrived at Mr. Doolittle's hotel. At first, he would vary some points every time he told it, which was, doubtless, owing to his having so recently awakened. It at last settled down to precisely the tale I have related, and there was not a man, woman, or child in the neighborhood but knew it by heart.

Some always pretended to doubt the reality of it, and insisted that Rip had been out of his head. The old Dutch inhabitants, however, almost all believed his story completely. Even to this day, they never hear a thunderstorm of a summer afternoon about the Catskills, but they say Hendrick Hudson and his crew are at their game of ninepins. And it is a common wish of all henpecked husbands in the neighborhood, when life hangs heavy on their hands, that they might have a quieting drink from Rip Van Winkle's flagon.

LEGEND OF SLEEPY HOLLOW or
The Headless Horseman

Sleepy Hollow

THERE IS a broad part of the Hudson River, which the ancient Dutch sailors called the Tappan Zee; and in a spacious cove of the Tappan Zee lies a small market town that is known by the name of Tarrytown. This name was given, we are told, by the good housewives of the countryside, because of their husbands' habit of tarrying in the village tavern. I do not know if it is true but merely report it to be exact.

Not far from this village, perhaps about two miles, there is a little valley among high hills, which is one of the quietest places in the whole world. A small brook glides through it, with just murmur enough to lull one to rest, and the occasional whistle of a quail or tapping of a woodpecker are almost the only sounds that ever break in upon the peace.

From the listless repose of the place and the peculiar character of its people — who are descendants of the original Dutch settlers — this little valley has long been known by the name of Sleepy Hollow.

A drowsy, dreamy air seems to hang over the valley. Some say that the place was bewitched during the early days of the settlement; others say that an old Indian chief, the prophet or wizard of his tribe, held his powwows there before the country was discovered by Master Hendrick Hudson.

Certain it is, there is still some witching power that holds a spell over the minds of the good people, causing them to walk in a continual daydream. They are given to all kinds of marvelous beliefs, are subject to trances and visions, frequently see strange sights, and hear music and voices in the air. The whole neighborhood abounds with local tales, haunted spots, and twilight superstitions; stars shoot and meteors glare oftener across Sleepy Hollow than in any other part of the country.

The spirit, however, that most often haunts this enchanted region is the apparition of a figure on horseback without a head. It is said by some to be the ghost of a Hessian trooper whose head had been carried away by a cannonball in some nameless battle during the Revolutionary War, and who is ever and anon seen by the country folk hurrying along in the gloom of the night as if on the wings of the wind. He haunts not only the valley, but at times the nearby roads, and especially a church at no great distance. Indeed, historians who have collected the floating facts about this specter claim that the body of the trooper was buried in the churchyard, that his ghost rides forth to the scene of battle in nightly quest of his head, and that the rushing speed with which he sometimes passes along the Hollow, like a midnight blast, is owing to his being late and in a hurry to get back to the churchyard before daybreak.

Such is the legendary superstition that has given rise to many a wild story in that region of shadows, and the specter is known at all the country firesides by the name of the Headless Horseman of Sleepy Hollow.

Ichabod Crane

In this dreamy byplace of nature there lived in a long-ago period of American history, a worthy man by the name of Ichabod Crane who stayed or, as he expressed it, "tarried" in Sleepy Hollow for the purpose of instructing the children. He was a native of Connecticut, a state that sends forth yearly legions of frontier woodsmen and country schoolmasters.

The name of Crane suited him. He was tall but exceedingly lank with narrow shoulders, long arms and legs, hands that dangled a mile out of his sleeves, and feet that might have served for shovels; his whole frame was most loosely hung together. His head was small and flat on top, and he had huge ears, large, green, glassy eyes, and a long, snip nose, so that it looked like a weathercock perched upon his spindle neck to tell which way the wind blew. Seeing him striding along the profile of a hill on a windy day, with his clothes bagging and fluttering about him, one might have mistaken him for some scarecrow eloped from a cornfield.

His schoolhouse was a low building of one large room, rudely constructed of logs, the windows partly patched with leaves of old copybooks. It was kept closed after school hours by a stick twisted through the handle of the door and stakes set against the window shutters, so that though a thief might get in with perfect ease, he might find some embarrassment in getting out.

The schoolhouse stood in a rather lonely but pleasant spot just at the foot of a woody hill, with a brook running close by and a huge birch tree growing at one end. From the school, the low murmur of pupils' voices saying over their lessons might be heard on a drowsy summer's day, sounding like the hum of a beehive. The murmur would be interrupted now and then by the commanding voice of the schoolmaster, or perhaps by the terrible sound of the birch rod as he urged some lazy student along the flowery path of knowledge. Truth to say, he was a conscientious man and he ever bore in mind the saying, "Spare the rod and spoil the child." Ichabod Crane's scholars certainly were not spoiled.

I would not have it imagined, however, that he was one of those cruel schoolmasters who find joy in the pain of their pupils. On the contrary, he administered justice as fairly as he could, easy on the weak and hard on the strong. A little child that drew back at the least movement of the rod was passed by with kindness, but a double portion would be given to any tough, wrong-headed urchin who sulked and swelled and grew mean. All this he called "doing his duty by their parents," and he never inflicted a punishment without following it by promising the smarting child that he would remember it and thank him for it the longest day he had to live.

But when school hours were over, Ichabod was often the companion and playmate of the larger boys, and on holiday afternoons would walk home with some of the smaller ones who happened to have pretty sisters or mothers noted for their good cooking. Indeed, he had to keep on good terms with his pupils. The pay from his school was small. It was scarcely enough to furnish him with daily bread, for he was a huge eater though thin. So, to help out with his keep, he stayed at the houses of the farmers whose children he instructed. With these he lived in turn, a week at a time, going the rounds of the neighborhood with all his worldly belongings tied up in a cotton handkerchief.

That all this might not be too hard on the purses of the parents, who were apt to consider the costs of schooling a burden and schoolmasters as mere drones, he had various ways of making himself both useful and agreeable. He helped the farmers occasionally in the lighter labors of their farms, helped to make hay, mended the fences, took the horses to water, drove the cows from pasture, and cut wood for the winter fire. He laid aside too his stern schoolroom manner and became wonderfully gentle and pleasant. He found favor in the eyes of the mothers by petting the children, particularly the youngest, and he would sit with a child on one knee and rock a cradle with his foot for whole hours together.

In addition to his other work, Ichabod was the singing master of the neighborhood and picked up extra money by instructing the young folk in the singing of hymns. On Sundays he liked to take his station in front of the church gallery with a band of chosen singers where, he thought, he received more attention than the parson. Certain it is, his voice resounded far above all the rest of the congregation.

Thus in many little ways, "by hook and by crook," the worthy teacher got on tolerably enough, and was thought by all who understood nothing of the labor of head work to have a wonderfully easy life of it.

The schoolmaster is generally a man of some importance in the female circle of a rural neighborhood, being considered a gentleman of much better taste and greater accomplishments than the rough country boys and, indeed, second in learning only to the parson. Therefore, there is apt to be a stir at the tea table of a farmhouse when he appears, and an extra dish of cakes or sweetmeats. A silver teapot may even be brought out.

Ichabod, therefore, was especially happy in the smiles of all the country girls. He would move among them in the churchyard between services on Sundays, gathering grapes for them from the wild vines that overran the surrounding trees, or reciting for their amusement all the epitaphs on the tombstones. Or he would saunter with a whole crowd of them along the banks of the millpond, while the more bashful country boys hung sheepishly back, envying his superior elegance.

Because of his wandering life, Ichabod was a kind of traveling newspaper, carrying the local gossip from house to house, so that his appearance was always greeted with satisfaction. He was, moreover, thought by the women to be very learned, for he had read several books quite through and was a perfect master of Cotton Mather's *History of New England Witchcraft,* in which, by the way, he most firmly believed.

He was, in fact, an odd mixture, being both rather clever and yet ready to believe anything. He loved stories of the marvelous and the supernatural and loved them even more since coming to this spellbound region. No tale was too much for him to swallow.

It was often his delight, after his school was dismissed in the afternoon, to stretch himself on the rich bed of clover bordering the little brook that whimpered by his schoolhouse. There he would pore over Mather's grim witch tales until the gathering dusk of the evening made the printed page a mere mist before his eyes. Then as he wended his way by swamp and stream and dim woodland to the farmhouse where he happened to be staying, every sound of nature at that witching hour fluttered his

excited imagination — the sound of the whippoorwill from the hillside; the boding cry of the tree toad foretelling a storm; the dreary hooting of the screech owl; or the sudden rustling in the thicket of birds frightened from their roost. Even the fireflies now and then startled him as one of uncommon brightness streamed across his path. And if, by chance, a huge blockhead of a beetle flew against him, poor Ichabod was ready to give up the ghost, thinking that he had been struck by a witch's token.

On such occasions, either to drown thought or drive away evil spirits, he would sing hymn tunes, and the good people of Sleepy Hollow, as they sat by their doors of an evening, were often filled with awe at hearing his nasal melody floating from the distant hill or along the dusky road.

Another of his sources of fearful pleasure was to pass long winter evenings with the old Dutch wives as they sat spinning by the fire, with a row of apples roasting and spluttering along the hearth. He would listen to their marvelous tales of ghosts and goblins, haunted fields, haunted brooks, haunted bridges, haunted houses, and particularly of the headless horseman. He in turn would delight them with his tales of witchcraft and of the awful omens and sights and sounds in the air in the earlier times of his native state of Connecticut. He would frighten them woefully with ideas about the meanings of comets and shooting stars and with the alarming fact that the world did absolutely turn around and that they were half the time topsy-turvy.

This telling of tales was pleasant while snugly cuddling in the chimney corner of a chamber that was all of a ruddy glow from the crackling wood fire and where, of course, no ghost dared to show its face.

But afterward, his walk homeward was filled with

terror. What fearful shapes and shadows beset his path amidst the dim and ghastly glare of a snowy night! With what wistful look did he eye every trembling ray of light streaming across the fields from some distant window! How often did he start at the sound of his own steps on the frosty crust beneath his feet and dread to look over his shoulder, lest he should behold some uncouth thing tramping close behind him! And how often was he thrown into complete dismay by some rushing blast howling among the trees, in the idea that it was the headless horseman on one of his nightly scourings! All these, however, were mere terrors of the night, phantoms of the mind that walk in darkness. Though he had been more than once beset by Satan in various shapes on his lonely walks, daylight put an end to all these evils.

Indeed, Ichabod would have passed a pleasant life if he had not finally met a being more perplexing than ghosts, goblins, and the whole race of witches put together, and that was — a woman.

Katrina Van Tassel

Among the young people who assembled each week to receive his instructions in music was Katrina Van Tassel, the daughter and only child of a rich

Dutch farmer. She was a blooming lass, just eighteen, plump as a partridge, ripe and melting and rosy-cheeked as one of her father's peaches, and universally famed not merely for her beauty but for her father's vast wealth. She was a bit of a coquette and beneath a provokingly short petticoat displayed the prettiest foot and ankle in the country round.

Ichabod Crane had a soft and foolish heart toward girls, and it is no wonder that this tempting morsel soon found favor in his eyes, especially after he had visited her in her father's home.

Old Baltus Van Tassel's farm was situated on the banks of the Hudson in one of those green, sheltered, fertile nooks which the Dutch farmers were so fond of settling. A great elm tree spread its broad branches over it, at the foot of which, in a little well, bubbled up a spring of the softest and sweetest water that stole sparkling away through the grass to a neighboring brook.

Near the farmhouse was a vast barn that seemed bursting with the treasures of the farm. The flail was busily resounding within it from morning to night; and on the roof rows of pigeons.

In the farmyard, sleek, unwieldy porkers were grunting in the peace and plenty of their pens, whence sallied forth now and then troops of suckling pigs. A stately squadron of snowy geese were riding in an adjoining pond, convoying whole fleets of ducks. Regiments of turkeys gobbled through the farmyard, and guinea fowls fretted about, like ill-tempered housewives, with their peevish, discontented cry.

Ichabod's mouth watered as he looked upon this sumptuous promise of wonderful winter meals. In his mind's eye, he pictured to himself every roasting-pig running about with an apple in its mouth. The pigeons were snugly put to bed in a comfortable pie and tucked in with a coverlet of crust. The geese were swimming in their own gravy and the ducks were paired cosily in dishes, like snug married couples, with a decent blanket of onion sauce. In the porkers, he seemed to see the future sleek side of bacon and juicy relishing ham. Each turkey he saw daintily trussed up with its gizzard under its wing and, perhaps, a necklace of savory sausages.

As the enraptured Ichabod fancied all this and as he rolled his great green eyes over the fat meadowlands, the rich fields of wheat, of rye, of buckwheat, and Indian corn, and the orchards burdened with ruddy fruit, which surrounded the warm homestead of Van Tassel, his heart yearned after the girl who was to inherit it all.

When Ichabod entered the house, the conquest of his heart was complete. It was one of those spacious farmhouses with high-ridged but low-sloping roofs, built in the style handed down from the first Dutch settlers, the low projecting eaves forming a piazza along the front capable of being closed up in bad weather. Under this were hung flails, harness, various tools of farming, and nets for fishing in the neighborhood river. Benches were built along the sides for summer use; and a great spinning wheel at one end and a churn at the other showed the various uses of this important porch.

From it, the wondering Ichabod entered the hall that formed the center of the mansion. Here rows of resplendent pewter, arranged on a long dresser, dazzled his eyes. In one corner stood a huge bag of wool ready to be spun, and in another, a quantity of linsey-woolsey fresh from the loom. Ears of Indian corn and strings of dried apples and peaches hung along the walls, mingled with gaudy red peppers. A door left ajar gave him a peep into the best parlor, where the claw-footed chairs and dark mahogany tables shone like mirrors and andirons glistened. Mock oranges and conch shells decorated the mantelpiece; strings of various-colored birds' eggs were suspended above it; a great ostrich egg was hung from the center of the room; and a corner cupboard, knowingly left open, displayed immense treasures of old silver and well-mended china.

From the moment Ichabod laid his eyes upon these regions of delight, his peace was at an end, and he became wholly concerned with how to gain the affections of the peerless daughter of Van Tassel.

In this, however, Ichabod had to deal with a host of fearful enemies — the numerous other young men who admired Katrina and who beat upon every door to her heart. These men kept a watchful and angry eye upon each other, but would band together against any new competitor.

Brom Bones

Among Katrina's admirers, the most fearsome was a burly, roaring, roistering fellow by the name of Abraham — or, according to the Dutch abbreviation, Brom — Van Brunt. He was the hero of the country round, which rang with his feats of strength and his hardihood. He was broad-shouldered and double-jointed, with short, curly black hair, and a bluff but not unpleasant face, having a mingled air of fun and arrogance. From his Herculean frame and great powers of limb, he had received the nickname of Brom Bones, by which he was universally known.

Brom was always ready for either a fight or a

frolic, but had more mischief than ill will and for all his overbearing roughness there was a strong dash of waggish good humor at bottom. He had three or four boon companions who regarded him as their model and with whom he scoured the country, attending every fight or party for miles around.

Sometimes Brom's crew would be heard dashing along past the farmhouses at midnight with whoop and halloo like a troop of Don Cossacks, and the old dames, startled out of their sleep, would listen for a moment till the hurry-scurry had clattered by, and then exclaim, "Ay, there goes Brom Bones and his gang!"

The neighbors looked upon him with a mixture of awe, admiration, and good will, and when any madcap prank or rustic brawl occurred in the vicinity, they always shook their heads and warranted Brom Bones was at the bottom of it.

Brom had for some time longed to win the blooming Katrina, and though his loving attentions were somewhat like the gentle caresses and endearments of a bear, it was whispered that she did not altogether discourage his hopes. Certain it is, his advances were signals for rivals to retire — if they felt no desire to challenge Brom. And when his horse was seen tied to Van Tassel's paling on a Sunday night, a sure sign that his master was courting within, all other suitors passed by in despair and went looking for other girls.

Such was Ichabod's formidable rival. A stouter man than he would have shrunk from the competition, and a wiser man would have given up. But Ichabod was both easy-going and persevering. He was like a supple branch, yielding but tough; though he bent, he never broke; and though he bowed beneath the slightest pressure, the moment it was away, jerk! — he was as erect and carried his head as high as ever.

Ichabod and Brom

To have gone openly against Brom would have been madness; for Brom was not a man to be beaten in love. Ichabod, therefore, made his advances in a quiet and gentle manner. As singing master, he made frequent visits to the farmhouse.

He never had anything to fear from meddlesome parents, which is so often a stumbling block in the path of lovers. Balt Van Tassel was an easy, indulgent soul; he loved his daughter better even than his pipe and, like a reasonable man and an excellent father, let her have her way in everything. His notable little wife too had enough to do to attend her housekeeping and manage her poultry. As she wisely observed, ducks and geese are foolish things and must be looked after, but girls can take care of themselves. Thus, while the busy Dame Van Tassel bustled about the house or plied her spinning wheel at one end of the piazza, honest Balt would sit smoking his evening pipe at the other, watching the weathervane spinning in the wind on the pinnacle of the barn.

In the meantime, Ichabod would talk with Katrina by the side of the spring under the great elm, or saunter along with her in the twilight, that hour so favorable to lovers.

Now Katrina was a coquette — flirting and fickle — easy enough to win, but not so easy to keep. And from the moment Ichabod Crane began to woo her, the fortunes of Brom Bones declined. His horse was no longer seen tied at the palings on Sunday nights, and a deadly feud gradually arose between him and the schoolmaster of Sleepy Hollow.

Brom would like to have settled the matter in the straightforward manner of the knights of old — by a single combat — but Ichabod was too conscious of Brom's superior strength to fight with him. He had overheard a boast of Bones that he would "double the schoolmaster up and lay him on a shelf of his own schoolhouse," and he was too wary to give him a chance.

There was something extremely provoking in Ichabod's stubborn peaceability; it left Brom no way of fighting except to play boorish, practical jokes upon his rival. Bones and his gang of rough riders smoked out Ichabod's singing school by stopping up the chimney; they broke into the schoolhouse at night, in spite of its fastenings, and turned everything topsy-turvy, so that the poor schoolmaster began to think all the witches in the country held their meetings there. But, what was still more annoying, Brom began to ridicule Ichabod in the presence of Katrina. Also, he had a mongrel dog, whom he taught to whine in the funniest manner, introducing him to Katrina as a rival of Ichabod's to instruct her in music. Matters went on this way for some time without changing Katrina's feelings about either of them.

One fine autumn afternoon, Ichabod, in a pensive mood, sat on the stool whence he usually watched over his schoolroom. In his hand he swayed a rod, while on the desk before him might be seen sundry articles and forbidden weapons taken from various idle pupils, such as half-munched apples, popguns, whirligigs, fly-cages, and whole legions of little paper game cocks. Apparently some dreadful punishment had recently taken place, for his scholars were all busy with their books or slyly whispering behind them with one eye kept upon the master. A kind of buzzing stillness reigned throughout the schoolroom.

It was suddenly interrupted by the appearance of a boy who came clattering up to the school door on the back of a half-broken colt with an invitation to Ichabod to attend a merrymaking or "quilting frolic" to be held that evening at Mynheer Van Tassel's.

All was now bustle and hubbub in the lately

quiet schoolroom. The scholars were hurried through their lessons without stopping at trifles. Those who were quick skipped over half without punishment, and those who were tardy felt a smart lick now and then in the rear to quicken their speed or help them over a tall word. Books were flung aside without being put away on the shelves, inkstands were over-turned, benches thrown down, and the whole school was turned loose an hour before the usual time bursting forth like a legion of young imps, yelping and racketing about in joy at their early freedom.

The gallant Ichabod now spent at least an extra half hour at his toilet, brushing and furbishing up his best — and, indeed, only — suit of rusty black, and arranging his hair by a bit of broken looking-glass that hung up in the schoolhouse. That he might make a dashing appearance, he borrowed a horse from the farmer with whom he was staying, a grouchy old Dutchman by the name of Hans Van Ripper, and, thus gallantly mounted, issued forth like a knight-errant in quest of adventures.

Ichabod and Gunpowder

But it is only fair that I should, in the true spirit of a romantic story, tell of the looks of my hero and his steed. The animal was a broken down plow horse that had outlived almost everything but his viciousness. He was bony and shaggy, with a crooked neck and a head like a hammer. His rusty mane and tail were tangled and knotted with burrs. One eye had lost its pupil, but the other had the gleam of a genuine devil in it. Still, he must have had fire and mettle in his day, if we may judge from his name: Gunpowder. He had, in fact, been a favorite of his master, the cross Van Ripper, who was a furious rider and had very probably given some of his own spirit to the animal. Old and broken down as Gunpowder looked, there was more of the lurking devil in him than in any young filly in the country.

Ichabod was a suitable figure for such a steed. He rode with short stirrups, which brought his knees nearly up to the pommel of the saddle. His sharp elbows stuck out like a grasshopper's. He carried his whip straight up like a wand, and as his horse jogged on, the motion of his arms was not unlike the flapping of a pair of wings. A small wool hat rested on the top of his nose (for so his scanty strip of forehead might as well be called), and the skirts of his black coat fluttered out almost to his horse's tail. Such was the appearance of Ichabod and his horse as they shambled out of the gate of Hans Van Ripper — altogether a sight seldom to be met in broad daylight.

The Party

It was toward evening that Ichabod arrived at the mansion of Mynheer Van Tassel, which he found thronged with the best people of the countryside. There were old farmers — a spare, leather-faced race — in homespun coats and breeches, blue stockings, and huge shoes with magnificent pewter buckles. Their brisk withered little dames wore close-crimped caps, long-waisted gowns, and homespun petticoats with scissors and pincushions and gay calico pockets hanging on the outside. The pretty lassies were almost as old-fashioned in their dress as their mothers, except where a straw hat, a fine ribbon, or perhaps a white frock gave symptoms of new city fashions. The sons were in short, square-skirted coats with rows of stupendous brass buttons, and their hair was generally tied back in the fashion of the times, especially if they could get an eelskin for the purpose. (An eelskin was esteemed throughout the country as a potent nourisher and strengthener of the hair.)

Brom Bones, however, was the hero of the scene, having come to the gathering on his favorite steed, Daredevil — a creature, like himself, full of mettle and mischief, which no one but himself could manage. Brom was, in fact, noted for preferring vicious animals given to all kinds of tricks, which kept the rider in constant risk of his neck; and he held a gentle well-broken horse as unworthy of a lad of spirit.

A world of charms burst upon the enraptured gaze of my hero, Ichabod, as he entered the state parlor of Van Tassel's mansion — not those of the pretty girls, but the ample charms of a genuine Dutch country tea table in the sumptuous time of autumn. Such heaped-up platters of various and almost indescribable kinds, known only to experienced Dutch housewives! There were doughty doughnuts, crisp and crumbling crullers, sweet cakes, short cakes, ginger cakes, and honey cakes — the whole family of cakes; and then there were apple pies, peach pies, and pumpkin pies, besides slices of ham and smoked beef; and moreover, delectable dishes of preserved plums and peaches and pears and quinces, not to mention broiled shad and roasted chicken, together with bowls of milk and cream — all mingled higgledy-piggledy, pretty much as I have enumerated them, with the motherly teapot sending up its clouds of vapor from the midst. Heaven bless the mark! I want breath and time to discuss this banquet as it deserves but am too eager to get on with my story. Happily, Ichabod Crane was not in so great a hurry as I and did ample justice to every dainty.

He was a kind and thankful creature, whose heart

swelled as his stomach was filled with good cheer, and whose spirits rose with eating as some men's do with drink. He could not help, too, rolling his large eyes as he ate, and chuckling with the possibility that he might one day be Katrina's husband and hence lord of all this scene of luxury and splendor. Then he thought how he would turn his back upon the old schoolhouse, snap his fingers in the face of Hans Van Ripper and every other stingy parent, and kick any wandering schoolteacher out of doors that should dare to call him comrade!

Old Baltus Van Tassel moved about among his guests with a face beaming with content and good humor, round and jolly as the harvest moon. His attentions were brief, but expressive — a shake of the hand, a slap on the shoulder, a loud laugh, and a pressing invitation to "fall to and help yourself."

Now the sound of the music from the common room, or hall, summoned all to dance. The musician was an old gray-headed fellow who had been the orchestra of the neighborhood for more than half a century. His instrument was as old and battered as himself. The greater part of the time he scraped on two or three strings, accompanying every movement of the bow with a motion of the head, bowing almost to the ground, and stamping with his foot whenever a fresh couple was to start.

Ichabod prided himself upon his dancing as much as upon his singing. Not a limb, not a fiber about him was idle. To see his loosely hung frame in full motion and clattering about the room, you would have thought that Saint Vitus himself, that blessed patron of the dance, was performing before you in person.

How could Ichabod be otherwise than animated and joyous? Katrina, the lady of his heart, was his partner in the dance; and she was smiling graciously at him, while Brom Bones, sorely smitten with love and jealousy, sat brooding by himself in one corner.

Tales of the Headless Horseman

When the dance was at an end, Ichabod joined a knot of the older folks who, with old Van Tassel, sat smoking at one end of the piazza, gossiping over former times and drawing out long stories about the war.

This neighborhood was one of those highly favored places that abound with history and great men. The British and American battle line had run near it during the Revolutionary War. It had been, therefore, the scene of many raids, and infested with refugees, cowboys, and all kinds of riff-raff. Just enough time had gone by to allow each story-teller to dress up his tale and to make himself the hero of every exploit.

But these stories were nothing to the tales of ghosts and apparitions that came later. There is no encouragement for ghosts in most of our villages. A ghost scarcely has time to finish his first nap and turn himself in his grave before his still-living friends have moved away from the neighborhood. So that when he turns out at night, he has no friends left to call upon. This is perhaps the reason why we so seldom hear of ghosts except in our old Dutch communities.

The immediate reason, however, was doubtless owing to the nearness of Sleepy Hollow and the very air that blew from that haunted region. It breathed forth an atmosphere of dreams and fancies, infecting all the land. Several of the Sleepy Hollow people were present at Van Tassel's and, as usual, were doling out their wild and wonderful legends. Many dismal tales were told about funeral trains, mourning cries, and wailings heard and seen, and of the woman in white that haunted the dark glen at Raven Rock and was often heard to shriek on winter nights before a storm, having died there in the snow. The chief part of the stories, however, turned upon the favorite specter of Sleepy Hollow, the headless horseman. Several times of late he had been patrol-

ling the country and, it was said, tethered his horse nightly among the graves in the churchyard.

The lonely situation of this church has always made it a favorite haunt of troubled spirits. To look upon its grass-grown yard, where the sunbeams seem to sleep so quietly, one would think that there, at least, the dead might rest in peace.

On one side of the church extends a wide, woody dell, along which flows a large brook among broken rocks and trunks of fallen trees. Over a deep, black part of the stream was a wooden bridge, and the bridge and the road that led to it were thickly shaded by overhanging trees. These cast a gloom about the place even in the daytime, but at night the trees made a fearful darkness. This was one of the favorite haunts of the headless horseman, and the place where he was most often seen.

The tale was told of old Brouwer, who did not believe in ghosts, and how he met the horseman returning from Sleepy Hollow. Brouwer was made to get up behind him, and they galloped over bush and brake, over hill and swamp, until they reached the bridge. There the horseman suddenly turned into a skeleton, threw old Brouwer into the brook, and sprang over the treetops with a clap of thunder.

This story was immediately matched by an adventure of Brom Bones, who said that on returning one night from the neighboring village of Sing-Sing, he had been overtaken by the horseman. Brom said that he had offered to race with him for a bowl of punch, and should have won it too for Daredevil beat the goblin horse all hollow. But just as they came to the church bridge, the horseman bolted and vanished in a flash of fire.

All these tales, told in that drowsy undertone with which men talk in the dark — the faces of the listeners gleaming only now and then in the glare of a pipe — sank deep into the mind of Ichabod. He repaid them with long stories from Cotton Mather, adding many events that had taken place in his native Connecticut, and fearful sights that he had seen in his nightly walks about Sleepy Hollow.

The Homeward Journey

The party now gradually broke up. The old farmers gathered their families together, and for some time their wagons could be heard rattling along the hollow roads and over the distant hills. Some of the girls mounted on horses behind their favorite young men. Their lighthearted laughter, mingling with the clatter of hoofs, echoed along the silent woodlands, sounding fainter and fainter until it gradually died away, and the late scene of noise and frolic was all silent and deserted. Only Ichabod lingered behind, according to the custom of country lovers, to speak with Katrina, certain that he was now on the high road to success.

What passed between them I will not pretend to say, for in fact I do not know. Something, however, I fear must have gone wrong, for Ichabod came out after a very short time with an air quite downcast. Oh these women! these women! Could that girl have been only playing the coquette? Was her encouragement of the poor teacher only a trick to help her win Brom? Heaven only knows, not I! But Ichabod stole forth with the air of one who has been stealing chickens, rather than a fair lady's heart. Without looking to the right or left, without even noticing the wealth of the Van Tassel farm over which he had so often gloated, he went straight to the stable, and with hearty cuffs and kicks roused his horse most uncourteously from his comfortable quarters.

It was the very witching time of night when

Ichabod, heavy-hearted and crestfallen, pursued his travel homeward along the sides of the lofty hills which rise above Tarrytown, and that he had traveled so cheerily in the afternoon. The hour was as dismal as himself. Far below him, the Tappan Zee spread its dusky and indistinct waste of waters, with here and there the tall mast of a sloop riding quietly at anchor. In the dead hush of midnight, he could even hear the barking of the watchdog from the opposite shore of the Hudson, so vague and faint as

only to reveal his distance from this faithful friend of man. Now and then, the long-drawn crowing of a cock, accidentally awakened, would sound far, far off, from some farmhouse away among the hills. There were no signs of life near him, but the occasional melancholy chirp of a cricket or the guttural twang of a bullfrog from a neighboring marsh.

All the stories of ghosts and goblins that he had heard in the afternoon now came crowding upon Ichabod's memory. The night grew darker and darker, the stars seemed to sink deeper in the sky, and driving clouds occasionally hid them from his sight. He had never felt so lonely and dismal. He was, moreover, approaching the very place where many of the scenes of the ghost stories had been laid. In the center of the road stood an enormous tree that towered like a giant above all the other trees of the neighborhood and formed a kind of landmark. Its limbs were gnarled and fantastic, large enough to form trunks for ordinary trees, twisting down almost to the earth and rising again into the air. The tree was connected with the tragic story of the English spy, André, who had been taken prisoner hard by and it was universally known as Major André's tree. The common people regarded it with a mixture of respect and superstition, partly because of the tales of strange sights and doleful cries told concerning it.

As Ichabod approached this fearful tree, he began to whistle. He thought his whistle was answered, but it was only a blast of wind sweeping sharply through the dry branches. As he approached a little nearer, he thought he saw something white hanging in the midst of the tree. He paused and stopped whistling, but on looking more narrowly, saw that it was a place where the tree had been struck by lightning and the white wood laid bare. Suddenly, he heard a groan. His teeth chattered, his knees knocked against the saddle, but it was merely the rubbing of one huge branch upon another as they swayed in the breeze. He passed the tree in safety, but new dangers lay before him.

About two hundred yards from the tree, a small brook crossed the road and ran into a marshy and thickly-wooded glen, known by the name of Wiley's Swamp. A few rough logs, laid side by side, served for a bridge over the stream. On the side of the road where the brook entered the wood, a group of oaks and chestnuts, matted thick with wild grapevines, threw a deep gloom over it. To pass this bridge was the worst trial. It was at this very spot that the unfortunate André was captured, and it was those very chestnut trees and vines that had concealed the men who surprised him. This has ever since been considered a haunted stream, and fearful are the feelings of the schoolboy who has to pass it alone after dark.

As he approached the stream, Ichabod's heart began to thump; he called up, however, all his courage, gave Gunpowder a dozen kicks in the ribs, and attempted to dash briskly across the bridge. But instead of starting forward, the stubborn old animal moved sidewise and ran broadside against the fence. Ichabod, whose fears grew worse with the delay, jerked the reins on the other side and kicked hard with the opposite foot. In vain; his horse started, it is true, but it was only to plunge to the opposite side of the road into a thicket of brambles and alder bushes. The schoolmaster now used both whip and heel upon the starved ribs of old Gunpowder, who dashed forward, snuffling and snorting, but came to a standstill just by the bridge, so suddenly he nearly sent his rider sprawling over his head.

Ichabod Meets the Headless Horseman

Just at this moment, a step by the side of the bridge caught Ichabod's sensitive ear. In the dark shadow of the grove, beside the brook, he beheld something huge, misshapen, black, and towering. It stirred not, but seemed gathered up into the gloom, like some gigantic monster ready to spring upon the traveler.

The hair of the terrified teacher stood on end. What was to be done? It was now too late to turn and fly; what chance was there of escaping ghost or goblin, if such it was, which could ride upon the wings of the wind? Summoning up, therefore, a show of courage, Ichabod demanded in stammering accents, "Who are you?" He received no reply. He repeated his demand in a still more terrified voice. Still there was no answer. Once more, he beat the sides of the unmovable Gunpowder and, shutting his eyes, began to sing a hymn.

Just then the shadowy thing began to move and with a scramble and a bound stood at once in the middle of the road. Though the night was dark and dismal, Ichabod could now partly make out the form of the thing. It appeared to be a horseman of large dimensions, mounted on a black horse of powerful frame. It made no attempt either to harm Ichabod or to be friendly, but kept to one side of the road, jogging along on the blind side of old Gunpowder, who had now gotten over his fright and waywardness.

Ichabod, who had no relish for this strange midnight companion (and began to think of the adventure of Brom Bones with the headless horseman), now quickened his steed in hopes of leaving him behind. The stranger, however, quickened his horse to an equal pace. Ichabod pulled up and fell into a walk, thinking to lag behind; the other did the same. The teacher's heart sank. He tried to resume his hymn tune, but his dry tongue stuck to the roof of his mouth, and he could not utter a line.

There was something in the moody and dogged silence of this companion that was both mysterious and appalling; and Ichabod soon discovered why. On mounting a rising ground, which brought the figure of his fellow traveler in relief against the sky, gigantic in height and muffled in a cloak, Ichabod was horror-struck to see that he was headless! But this horror grew when he saw that the head, which should have rested on his shoulders, was carried before him on the saddle.

His terror rose to desperation; he rained a shower of kicks and blows upon Gunpowder, hoping to give his companion the slip, but the ghost started full jump with him. Away, then, they dashed through thick and thin, stones flying, and sparks flashing at every bound. Ichabod's flimsy garments fluttered in the air as he stretched his long lanky body way over his horse's head in the eagerness of his flight.

They had now reached the road that turns off to Sleepy Hollow; but Gunpowder, who seemed possessed with a demon, instead of staying on it, made an opposite turn and plunged headlong downhill to the left. This road leads through a sandy hollow shaded by trees for about a quarter of a mile, where it crosses the bridge famous in goblin story; and just beyond swells the green knoll on which stands the whitewashed church.

As yet the panic of the horse had given Ichabod a small advantage in the chase; but just as he had got halfway through the hollow, the girths of the saddle gave way, and he felt it slipping from under him. He seized it by the pommel and tried to hold it firm, but it was no use. He had just time to save himself by clasping old Gunpowder round the neck before the saddle fell to the earth, and he heard it trampled underfoot by the ghostly horseman. For a moment, the terror of Hans Van Ripper's fury passed across his mind, for it was Van Ripper's Sunday saddle. But this was no time for petty fears; the goblin was almost on his haunches, and, unskilled rider that he was, it was all he could do to keep his seat. Sometimes he slipped to one side, sometimes to the other, and sometimes he was jolted on the high ridge of his horse's backbone so hard that he truly feared he would be cloven in half.

An opening in the trees now cheered him with the hope that the church bridge was at hand. The wavering reflection of a silver star in the brook told him that he was not mistaken. He saw the walls of the church dimly glaring under the trees beyond. He recollected the place where Brom Bones had seen the headless horseman disappear. "If I can but reach that bridge," thought Ichabod, "I am safe."

Just then he heard the black steed panting and blowing close behind him. He even fancied that he felt his hot breath. Another mighty kick in the ribs, and old Gunpowder sprang upon the bridge, he thundered over the resounding planks; he gained the opposite side; and now Ichabod cast a look behind to see if the horseman should vanish, according to Brom's story, in a flash of fire and brimstone.

Just then he saw the goblin rising in his stirrups and in the very act of hurling his head at him. Ichabod tried to dodge the horrible thing, but too late. The ghost's head met his own with a tremendous crash. He was thrown headlong into the dust, and Gunpowder, the black steed, and the goblin rider passed like a whirlwind.

The Disappearance of Ichabod Crane

The next morning, the old horse was found, without his saddle and with the bridle under his feet, soberly cropping the grass at his master's gate. Ichabod did not make his appearance at breakfast; dinner hour came, but no Ichabod. The boys assembled at the schoolhouse and strolled idly about the banks of the brook, but no schoolmaster. Hans Van Ripper now began to feel some uneasiness about the fate of poor Ichabod and his own saddle.

The neighbors began to look for Ichabod, and at last they came upon his traces. In one part of the road leading to the church was found the saddle, trampled in the dirt. The tracks of horses' hoofs, deeply dented in the road and evidently at furious speed, were traced to the bridge, beyond which, on the bank of a broad part of the brook where the water ran deep and black, was found the hat of the unfortunate Ichabod. Close behind it was a shattered pumpkin. The brook was searched, but the body of the schoolmaster was not to be discovered.

Later, Hans Van Ripper examined the bundle that contained all Ichabod's worldly effects. They consisted of a few clothes, a rusty razor, a dog-eared book of hymn tunes, and a broken pitch pipe. The books and furniture of the schoolhouse belonged to the community, excepting Cotton Mather's *History of Witchcraft,* a *New England Almanac,* and a book of dreams and fortune-telling. In the last was a sheet of paper much scribbled and blotted in several fruitless attempts to write some verses in honor of Katrina Van Tassel. These magic books and the poetic scribbles were at once thrown into the flames by Hans Van Ripper, who from that time forward decided never again to send his children to school, saying that he never knew any good to come of reading and writing. Whatever money the schoolmaster possessed, and he had received his quarter's pay but a day or two before — he must have had with him when he disappeared.

The mysterious event caused much talk at the church on the following Sunday. Knots of gazers and gossips were collected in the churchyard, at the bridge, and at the spot where the hat and pumpkin had been found. The stories of Brouwer, of Bones, and of others were called to mind, and when they had talked them all over and compared them with the clues of the present case, they shook their heads and decided that Ichabod had been carried off by the headless horseman. As he was a bachelor and in nobody's debt, nobody troubled his head any more about him. The school was removed to a different quarter of the hollow, and another teacher ruled in his stead.

It is true that an old farmer, who had been down to New York on a visit several years after, brought home the news that Ichabod Crane was still alive; that he had left the neighborhood, partly through fear of the goblin and Hans Van Ripper, and partly in shame at having been suddenly turned away by Katrina; that he had moved to a distant part of the country; that he had kept school and studied law at the same time, had been admitted to the bar, turned politician, electioneered, written for the newspapers, and finally had been made a justice of the Ten Pound Court.

Brom Bones, who shortly after Ichabod's disappearance led the blooming Katrina in triumph to the altar, was seen to look very knowing whenever the story of Ichabod was told. He always burst into a hearty laugh at the mention of the pumpkin, which led some to suspect that he knew more about the matter than he chose to tell.

The old country wives, however, who are the best judges of these matters, maintain to this day that Ichabod was spirited away by supernatural means; and it is a favorite story often told about the neighborhood, round the winter evening fire.

The bridge became more than ever an object of superstition and fear, and that may be the reason why the road has been changed of late years, so as to approach the church by the border of the mill pond. The schoolhouse, being deserted, soon fell to decay, and was reported to be haunted by the ghost of the unfortunate schoolmaster; and the plowboy, wandering homeward of a still summer evening, has often fancied hearing Ichabod's voice at a distance, chanting a melancholy hymn tune in the lonely quiet of Sleepy Hollow.